Once, when I was six, I saw an amazing picture in a book all about the primeval forest, called "True Stories". It showed a boa constrictor swallowing a wild animal.

"Boa constrictors swallow their prey whole, without chewing. They can't move after that, and it takes them six months to sleep off their meal."

That got me thinking.

Around that time I did my first drawing.

It looked like this.

1

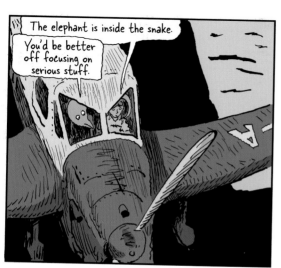

Thce

ADAPTED XUPÉRY

TRANSLATED BY SARAH ARDIZZONE

COLOURS BY BRIGITTE FINDAKLY

WALKER

For Sandrina
J.S.

First published in France as *Le Petit Prince: D'Après L'Œvre
d'Antoine de Saint-Exupéry* by Gallimard Jeunesse

First published in the UK 2010 by Walker Books Ltd
87 Vauxhall Walk, London SE11 5HJ

This paperback edition published in the UK 2013 by Walker Books Ltd

10 9 8 7 6 5 4 3 2 1

Text and illustrations © 2008 Gallimard Jeunesse
English translation © 2010 Sarah Ardizzone

This book has been typeset in Skippy Sharp

Printed in China

British Library Cataloguing in Publication Data:
a catalogue record for this book is available from the British Library

ISBN 978-1-4063-3198-1

www.walker.co.uk

Grown-ups told me to give up drawing.

Grown-ups never understand anything by themselves.

I've lived among grown-ups a lot. I've seen them close up. And they still don't impress me.

I talk to them about bridge, about golf, about politics and about knotting a tie.

But never about boa constrictors.

They don't have anything interesting to say to each other.

4

5

But...

What are you doing here?

Please,
draw me a sheep.

6

7

9

That's just how I wanted him.

Do you think this sheep will need a lot of grass?

Why?

Because it's very small where I come from.

I'm sure there'll be enough grass. I've given you a very small sheep.

He's not that small...

Look! He's fallen asleep.

11

What's good about the box you gave me is that, at night, it can be the sheep's house.

So where do you come from?

Where are you planning to take my sheep?

He'll sleep in the box you gave me.

It can be his house.

Of course.

And I'll give you a rope, as well, to tie him up during the day.

13

14

17

18

19

20

You had a bad dream.

Yes. There were baobabs everywhere.

Go back to sleep, you don't need to be afraid of baobabs tonight.

Oh yes, I do.

Look around you. Nothing grows here.

Not here, no.

But where I come from, it's different.

Things can grow while I'm not there. Perhaps that'll all change, thanks to the sheep.

Why?

Because I think sheep eat small shrubs.

I'm sure you're right.

21

CRRRR ... yes ... we need an emergency rescue team ... 633t...

Red alert ...CRRRR ... baobab seeds everywhere ... nobody to pull them out...

They grow, they infest everything aaaand

CRAAAAACK!
The planet in smithereens.

Who are you talking to?

Nobody.

The radio's broken, so I'm playing around.

Can I join in? Pleeease!

23

24

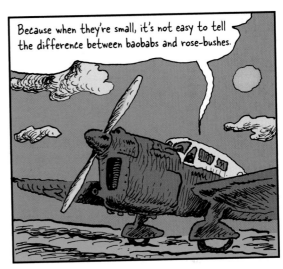

Children, beware of baobabs.

They've got invisible seeds that sleep in the earth's secret hiding-place — until one of them chooses to wake up.

At which point it stretches up and sends out a beautiful, harmless shoot in the direction of the sun.

If it's a radish or a rose-bush shoot, you can let it grow as it likes.

But if it's a weed, you have to pull it out straight away.

Children, beware of baobabs.

26

On the morning of the fourth day after the accident, the little prince said to me:

I really like sunsets.

Let's go and watch a sunset.

We'll have to wait.

What for?

For the sun to go to bed.

You're right. I keep thinking I'm back home.

Where I come from, I once watched the sun setting forty-four times in a day.

You see, when you're feeling very sad, you like sunsets.

Were you feeling very sad, on the day of forty-four sunsets?

Day 5. I wasn't getting anywhere with mending my aeroplane. I didn't have much water left.

If a sheep eats shrubs, does that mean it'll eat flowers too?

A sheep eats anything it comes across.

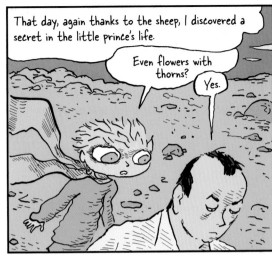

That day, again thanks to the sheep, I discovered a secret in the little prince's life.

Even flowers with thorns?

Yes.

So what do thorns do?

Hey! I asked you a question.

Thorns don't do anything.

They're just flowers being spiteful. Now let me get on with my work.

29

If flowers have been growing thorns for millions of years, and they still get eaten by sheep, that's serious.

Why do they go to so much trouble to grow useless thorns?

I know a planet with a man on it who's never loved anybody. He does sums all day long and he claims that's serious.

Stop.

If I don't mend my aeroplane, my life will stop.

Do you understand?

I know a flower you won't find anywhere else, apart from on my planet.

Out of all the millions and millions of stars, there's only one of her.

And when I look at the sky, I say to myself: "My flower is out there somewhere!"

And that's all I need to make me happy. Imagine if a sheep ate her by mistake.

It would be like all the stars going out at once.

Don't you think that's serious?

3.

He couldn't speak any more. He burst into tears.

There was a little prince to console on Earth.

I took him in my arms. I cradled him.

I told him: "The flower you love isn't in danger."

I'll draw a muzzle for your sheep.

And I'll draw a fence for your flower.

...I...

There'd always been very simple flowers on the little prince's planet, which didn't take up any room or disturb anybody.

They would appear one morning in the grass, and fade away in the evening.

But this one had sprouted one day out of a seed from who knows where. The little prince had watched very closely over its stem, which didn't look like any other stem.

The little prince watched an enormous bud getting ready, and he could tell that it would produce a miracle.

But the flower just kept on making herself beautiful, in the shelter of her green bedroom. She chose her colours carefully.

She was getting dressed slowly.

3.

She adjusted her petals one by one. She didn't want to come out crumpled like poppies do.

She wanted to appear in the full radiance of her beauty.

That was why she spent days and days mysteriously getting washed and dressed.

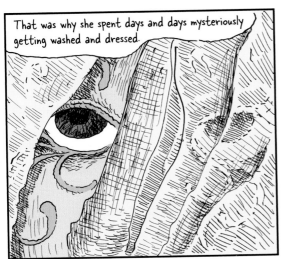

Then one morning as the sun was rising she revealed herself.

And the flower, who had worked on every last detail, yawned and said:

Ah! I've only just woken up.

You'll have to forgive me. My hair's in a mess.

The flower quickly tormented him with her prickly vanity. One day, for instance, while she was talking about her four thorns, she said to the little prince:

I'm ready for those tigers, with their claws!

There aren't any tigers on my planet.

And anyway, tigers don't eat weeds.

I'm not a weed.

I'm sorry.

I'm not afraid of tigers, but I can't bear draughts. You wouldn't have a screen, by any chance?

How's that?

Hmmm ... no. I want a proper screen.

Every evening, you must keep me under a glass cover. It's very cold on your planet.

37

And it's uncomfortable too. Where I come from—

You don't come from anywhere.

You were born yesterday.

I didn't mean to upset you.

Cough! Cough! Is that screen coming?

I was about to go and look for it, but you were talking to me.

Cough! Cough!

And so, despite being keen to love his flower, the little prince had quickly come to doubt her.

He'd taken words seriously that didn't matter at all, and he'd become very unhappy.

I shouldn't have listened to her. Never listen to flowers. Just look, and breathe in their scent.

The scent of my flower filled my whole planet, but I didn't know how to enjoy it. Her stories about tigers and draughts should have melted my heart, not irritated me.

I shouldn't have run away! I should have realized that she was fond of me, behind her wily tricks.

But I was too young to know how to love her.

39

I believe he escaped with some migrating wild birds.

On the morning he left, he tidied up his planet. He cleaned out his active volcanoes carefully.

He had an extinct volcano too. But, as he said, "you never know."

So he cleaned out the extinct volcano as well.

On the Earth, you're too small to clean out your volcanoes. That's why ...

... they're such a bother.

41

The flower coughed, but it wasn't because of her cold.

I've been very silly, I'm sorry.

Try to be happy.

Don't worry about the glass dome, I don't want it any more.

But ... what about the wind?

I haven't got that much of a cold. The cool evening air will do me good. I'm a flower.

But ... what about the insects?

I'll have to put up with two or three caterpillars, if I want to meet some butterflies. Otherwise, who'll pay me a visit?

You'll be so far away.

42

Don't dawdle. Off you go.

She didn't want him to see her crying.

She was such a proud flower.

I love you.

Perhaps it's my fault that you didn't understand. You're as foolish as I am.

Oh, what does it matter?

43

The little prince was in the region of asteroids 325, 326, 327, 328, 329 and 330.

So he began by visiting them, to find out what he might like to do, and to learn a thing or two.

The first was inhabited by a king.

Dressed in purple and ermine, the king was sitting on a throne that was simple but majestic.

Oh!

Here comes a subject.

How do you know I'm your subject, when we've never met?

Everyone's my subject.

OH...

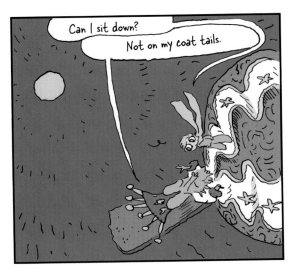

45

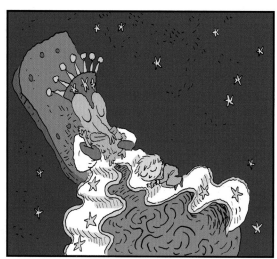

48

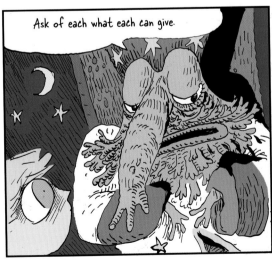

48

49

Here's an idea! I think there's an old rat somewhere on my planet. I can hear it at night.

Scratch! Scratch! You could judge it, if you liked. You could sentence it to death, from time to time. And then pardon it, so as not to waste it.

Because there's only one.

That way, its life would depend on your justice.

I don't want to sentence anyone to death.

And I think I'll be on my way now.

NO

If Your Majesty wishes to be obeyed promptly, he could give me a sensible command. For example, he could command me to leave within the minute.

The conditions look favourable.

I'll make you an ambassador.

Grown-ups are very strange.

The second planet was inhabited by a vain man. "Ah! Ah! Here comes an admirer!" the vain man called out, as soon as he spotted the little prince at a distance.

Aha!

Because for vain people, everyone else is an admirer.

Here comes an admirer.

Hello.

You've got a funny hat.

It's so I can greet the cheering crowds.

Unfortunately, nobody ever comes this way.

Oh?

Clap your hands together.

Clap! Clap! Clap!

There you go.

I mean, really,

grown-ups

are very odd...

55

56

Three plus two makes five. Five plus seven, twelve.

The fourth planet belonged to a businessman.

Twelve plus three, fifteen.

Hello.

Bzzzzz

He was so busy, he didn't even look up when the little prince arrived.

Fifteen plus seven, twenty-two. Twenty-two plus six, twenty-eight.

Your cigarette's gone out.

No time to light it again.

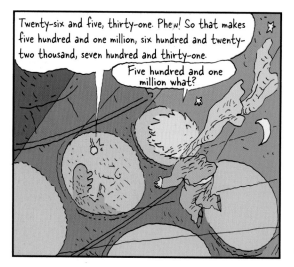

Twenty-six and five, thirty-one. Phew! So that makes five hundred and one million, six hundred and twenty-two thousand, seven hundred and thirty-one.

Five hundred and one million what?

Uh? Are you still here? Five hundred and one million ... I can't remember now.

I've got so much work! I'm a serious person. I don't do small talk! Two and five, seven—

Five hundred and one million what?

I've lived on this planet for fifty-four years, and I've only been disturbed three times. The first time was twenty-two years ago, by a beetle making a terrible racket, and I made four mistakes adding up.

The second time was eleven years ago, because of my rheumatism.

Now where was I, five hundred and one million—

Millions of what?

Millions of those little things you sometimes see in the sky.

Flies?

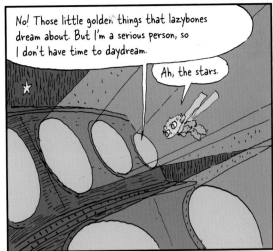

No! Those little golden things that lazybones dream about. But I'm a serious person, so I don't have time to daydream.

Ah, the stars.

That's right. The stars.

Five hundred and one million, six hundred and twenty-two thousand, seven hundred and thirty-one. I'm serious, me, and accurate too.

And what do you do with five hundred and one million stars?

Nothing. I own them.

What's the point of that?

To be rich.

I've already seen a king who—

Irrelevant! Kings "reign". They don't own. It's quite different.

And what's the point of being rich?

To buy more stars, if somebody finds them.

This man thinks along similar lines to the drunkard, observed the little prince.

How can anyone own stars?

Who do they belong to?

Nobody.

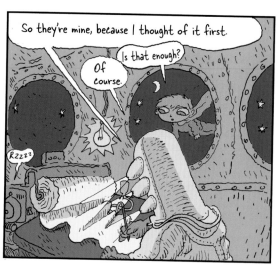

So they're mine, because I thought of it first.

Of course.

Is that enough?

Rzzzz

When you find a diamond that doesn't belong to anybody, it's yours. When you find an island that doesn't belong to anybody, it's yours. When you're the first person to have an idea, you patent it and it's yours.

And I own the stars, because nobody thought of it before me.

I suppose that's true.

But what do you do with them?

I manage them. I count them and then I count them again. It's a serious business.

If I owned a scarf, I could wear it around my neck and take it with me. If I owned a flower, I could pluck it and take it with me. But you can't pluck the stars.

No. But I can put them in a bank.

What does that mean?

I write down how many stars I've got, on a small piece of paper. And then I lock that piece of paper away in a drawer.

That's all?

Yes.

That's funny.

It's quite poetic, but it's not very serious.

I have a flower I water every day and three volcanoes I clean out every week. I'm useful to my volcanoes and my flower.

But you, you're not useful to the stars.

The fifth planet was the smallest of all. There was just enough room for a street lamp.

The little prince couldn't see the point of a street lamp and a lamp lighter on a planet without houses or people.

Perhaps this man is simply absurd.

Then again, he's less absurd than the king, or the vain man, or the businessman or the drinker. At least his work has a purpose.

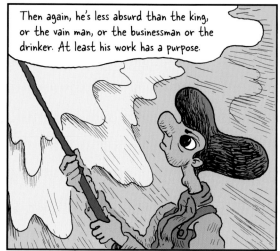

When he lights his street lamp, it's as if he's creating another star, or a flower. And when he extinguishes the street lamp, it puts the flower or the star to sleep. Which is a beautiful thing to do.

It's useful because it's beautiful.

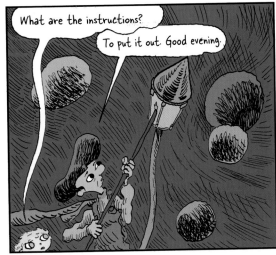

63

It was fair enough in the old days. I would put the lamp out in the morning and light it in the evening. I had the rest of the day to relax and the rest of the night to sleep...

Have the instructions changed since then?

No, the instructions haven't changed. That's the problem.

This planet has been spinning faster and faster, year on year, but the instructions haven't changed.

So?

So now it does a complete rotation every minute, and I don't get a second to relax. I light up and put it out once a minute!

How funny! Where you live, the days last a minute!

It's not funny at all.

6

We've already been talking for a month.

A month?

Yes. Thirty minutes. Thirty days!

Good evening!

The little prince watched the lamp lighter and he liked the way he was so faithful to the instructions.

He remembered the sunsets he used to try to catch, by moving his chair. He wanted to help his friend:

Your planet is so small you can get around it in three strides. Just walk slowly and you'll stay in the sun all day.

The day will last for as long as you keep walking.

That wouldn't help me much. What I enjoy in life is sleeping.

How unlucky.

Yes, how unlucky. Good morning.

And he put out his street lamp.

He'd be looked down on by all the others. By the king, by the vain man, by the drinker, by the businessman.

But, if you ask me, he's the only one who isn't ridiculous.

Perhaps it's because he looks after something apart from himself. He's a friend. But his planet really is too small.

No room for two people.

The sixth planet was ten times the size. On it lived an old gentleman who wrote enormous books.

Goodness me! Here comes an explorer!

Where have you come from?

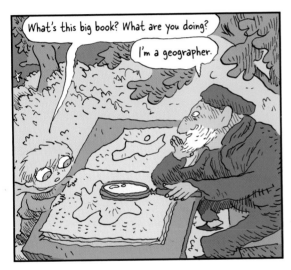

What's this big book? What are you doing?

I'm a geographer.

What's that?

I study where the seas and rivers are, and the towns, mountains and deserts too.

That's very interesting!

At last, a proper profession.

Because drunkards see double. So the geographer would record two mountains instead of one.

I know somebody who would make a bad explorer.

That's quite possible. Anyway, when the explorer seems of sound moral character, we investigate what he's discovered.

Do you go and see it?

No, that would be too complicated.

We ask the explorer to bring back some proof. For example, if he says he's discovered a big mountain, we ask him to bring back some big stones... Hold on ...

... you've come from far away! You're an explorer! Describe your planet for me.

I'll write in pencil first, you understand...

I'll ink it in when you've provided me with some proof.

My flower is shortly in danger of disappearing?

Of course.

My flower is ephemeral, thought the little prince. She's only got four thorns to defend herself against the world! And I left her all alone on my planet!

This was the first time he'd felt any regrets. But he plucked up courage again.

Where would you recommend I visit?

Planet Earth. It has a good reputation.

And off the little prince went, dreaming of his flower.

And so the seventh planet was Earth.

71

Earth isn't just any old planet! You can count one hundred and eleven kings, seven thousand geographers, nine hundred thousand businessmen, seven and a half million drunkards, and three hundred and eleven million vain people on it.

Which makes about two billion grown-ups.

To give you an idea of the Earth's dimensions, let me tell you that before electricity was invented, they had to keep an army of four hundred and sixty-two thousand, five hundred and eleven lamp lighters, across the six continents.

Seen from a little way off, it was quite a spectacle.

So once the little prince reached the Earth, he was very surprised not to see anybody.

He was beginning to worry he'd got the wrong planet, when a moon-coloured snake shifted in the sand.

73

Where are all the people? It feels a bit lonely in the desert.

It can be lonely among people too.

You're a funny animal, no thicker than a finger.

But I'm more powerful than the finger of a king.

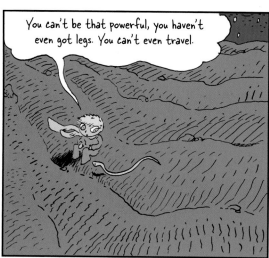

You can't be that powerful, you haven't even got legs. You can't even travel.

I can transport you further than any ship.

He wound himself around the little prince's ankle, like a golden bracelet.

I can send any person I touch back to the earth they came from.

But you're pure and come from a star. You're so fragile, I feel sorry for you on this granite Earth.

The little prince climbed to the top of a high mountain.

From a mountain as high as this, I'll be able to see the whole planet and all the people, at a glance...

But all he could see were rocks sharp as needles.

HELLO

Hello

Hello

Hello

Who are you?

"Who are you ... who are you ... who are you..." came the echo.

Please be my friends, I'm all alone.

People have no imagination. They just repeat what you say to them. I had a flower on my planet, and she always spoke first.

I'm all alone...

I'm ... all alone ...

... I'm all alone...

After walking for a long time across sand, rock and snow, the little prince found a road at last. And all roads lead to people.

Hello

It was a garden adorned with roses.

Hello

Hello

Hello

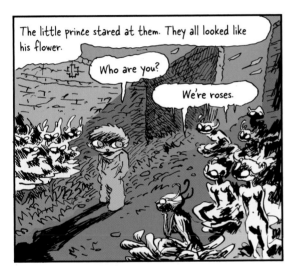

The little prince stared at them. They all looked like his flower.

Who are you?

We're roses.

And he felt terribly sad.

She'd be so upset if she could see this.

His flower had told him there was only one rose like her in the universe.

She'd have to cough a lot and pretend to be dying, so as not to look foolish. And I'd have to pretend to make her better.

Otherwise, to humiliate me too, she really would let herself die.

77

I used to think I had a special flower that made me rich, but all I've got is an ordinary rose.

That and three volcanoes, which only come up to my knees, and one of them's probably extinct anyway.

That doesn't make me a very great prince.

He lay in the grass and wept.

Just then, the fox appeared.

Hello.

Hello?

I'm here. Under the apple tree.

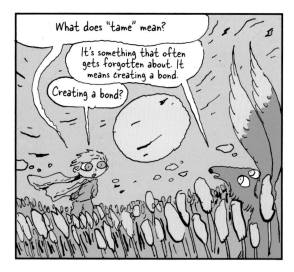

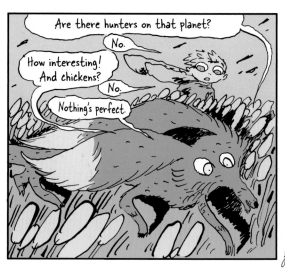

But the fox went back to what he was saying.

I lead a dull life. I hunt chickens, and people hunt me. All the hens look the same and all the people look the same. So I get a bit bored.

But if you tame me, there'll be sunshine in my life. I'll recognize a footstep that sounds different from all the rest. Everyone else's footsteps send me underground. But yours will be like music calling me out of my den.

And look! You see those wheat fields over there? Wheat is of no use to me, it doesn't remind me of anything. But you've got hair the colour of gold. So it'll be fantastic when you tame me. The golden wheat will remind me of you.

And I'll enjoy the sound of the wind in the wheat.

Please. Tame me!

I'd like to, but I don't have much time. I've got new friends to make and a lot to understand.

We only understand what we tame.

If you want a friend, tame me.

What do I have to do?

Be very patient.

To start with you'll sit a little way off from me, like that, in the grass. I'll watch you out of the corner of my eye and you won't say a word. Misunderstandings spring from language.

But each day, you'll be able to sit a bit closer.

The next day the little prince came back.

It's best to come back at the same time. For instance, if you come at four o'clock in the afternoon, I'll start feeling happy from three o'clock.

But if you come at any old time, I won't know when to get my heart ready. That's why we need rituals.

The little prince went off to see the roses again.

You don't look anything like my rose, you're nothing yet.

Nobody's tamed you and you haven't tamed anybody.

Nobody would die for you.

Of course, an ordinary passer-by might think my rose looks like you.

But she's more important than all of you.

She's the one I watered
She's my rose.

Then he headed back to the fox.

Goodbye.

Goodbye. Here's my secret. It's very simple.

You can only see clearly with the heart. What matters is invisible to the eye.

What matters is invisible to the eye.

It's the time you've given up for your rose that makes your rose so important.

It's the time I've given up for my rose.

You'll always be responsible for what you've tamed. You're responsible for your rose...

"I'm responsible for my rose," the little prince repeated, so as not to forget.

One day, I saw a man selling clever pills for quenching thirst. If you swallow one a week you don't get thirsty any more.

He said it saved you time. Just think, we spend fifty-three minutes a week drinking.

I told him that if I had fifty-three minutes to spend, I would walk very slowly towards a fountain.

I like hearing your memories, but I still haven't mended my aeroplane.

I haven't got anything left to drink and, like you, there's nothing I'd like more than to walk very slowly towards a fountain.

My friend the fox—

My little friend, it's not about the fox any more!

Why?

Because we're going to die of thirst...

It's good to have had a friend, even if you're about to die. I'm glad I had a fox for a friend.

"He doesn't realize the danger," I thought to myself. "He's never hungry or thirsty. A little sunshine is enough for him."

But he looked at me and answered my thoughts.

I'm thirsty too ... let's look for a well...

I made a weary gesture: it's crazy to go looking for a well on the off chance, in the vastness of the desert. But we set out walking.

So you're thirsty too?

Water can also be good for the heart.

I didn't understand his answer, but I kept quiet. There was no point in asking him questions.

He was tired. He sat down. I sat down next to him. And after a while, he said:

The stars are beautiful because of a flower we can't see.

"Of course," I answered, and, without saying another word, I looked at the ridges of sand under the moon.

What makes the desert even more beautiful is the fact that it's hiding a well somewhere.

Yes. When I was a little boy, I used to live in a very old house, and legend had it that treasure was buried there. Nobody ever found it, but it made the whole house seem enchanted.

My house hid a secret deep in its heart. Yes, whether it's a house, or the stars, or the desert, what makes them beautiful is something invisible.

I'm glad.

Because you agree with my fox.

The little prince had drifted off to sleep, so I took him in my arms and continued on my way.

I was deeply moved.

I felt I was carrying a fragile treasure.

In fact, I felt there was nothing more fragile on Earth.

In the moonlight, I stared at that pale forehead, those closed eyes, his locks of hair trembling in the breeze.

And I said to myself: "What I can see here is only the outer shell.

The most important part is invisible."

89

As his parted lips sketched a half-smile, I said to myself again: "What's so touching about the little sleeping prince, is how faithful he is to a flower ...

... the image of a rose shines in him like a lamp, even when he's asleep."

And I sensed him becoming even more fragile.

I kept on walking, and I discovered the well at sunrise.

The well didn't look like a Saharan well. Saharan wells are simple holes dug into the sand.

This one looked like a village well. But there wasn't any village, so I thought I was dreaming.

He laughed, held the rope and set the pulley in motion.

Let me do that, it's too heavy for you.

Slowly, I hoisted the bucket up to the edge of the well. I set it down carefully.

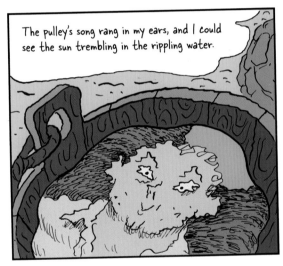

The pulley's song rang in my ears, and I could see the sun trembling in the rippling water.

I'm thirsty for that water. Give me some to drink.

And I understood what he'd been looking for! I tilted the bucket to his lips. He drank, with his eyes closed.

It was sweet as a celebration. That water was more than just a drink.

It was born from our walking under the stars, from the pulley's song, from my straining arms.

Like a gift, it was good for the heart.

I had drunk. I was breathing easily. The sand at daybreak is honey-coloured.

An uplifting honey colour.

So why did I have this sad feeling...

95

Next to the well was the ruin of an old stone wall. When I returned after work the following evening, I saw my little prince up there, legs dangling. And I could hear him talking.

Don't you remember? It's not quite here.

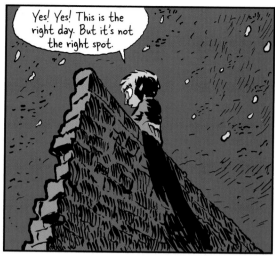

Yes! Yes! This is the right day. But it's not the right spot.

Of course. You'll see where my footsteps begin in the sand. Just wait for me. I'll be there tonight.

Have you got some good venom? You're sure you won't make me suffer too long?

I came to a halt, my heart heavy, but I still didn't understand.

Now go away, I want to climb down again.

Then I looked down at the foot of the wall and gave a startled jump. There, rising up towards the little prince, was one of those yellow snakes that can kill you in a matter of seconds.

Groping in my pocket for my revolver, I chased after it.

But with all the noise I was making, the snake slipped off into the sand, like a fountain spray drying up.

I reached the wall just in time to catch my little prince,

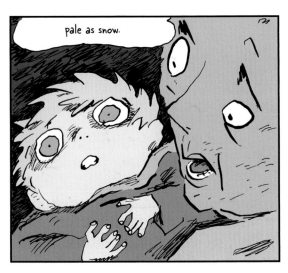

pale as snow.

Why are you talking to snakes?

97

I had undone the golden scarf the little prince always wore. I'd wetted his temples and got him to drink.

And now I didn't dare ask him anything else. He gave me a serious look and wrapped his arms round my neck.

I could feel his heart beating like that of a dying bird, shot with a rifle.

I'm glad you found out what was missing from your machine.

You'll be able to go back to where you come from.

How did you know?

Sure enough, I'd come to tell him that, against all odds, my work had been successful.

I'm going back to where I come from today too.

But it's much further. And much more difficult.

I hugged him in my arms like a small child, but he seemed to be slipping down into an abyss, and there was nothing I could do to hold him back.

His expression was very serious, his eyes lost in the distance.

I've got your sheep. And I've got the box for the sheep. And the muzzle too.

I waited for a long time. I could feel him slowly warming up.

My poor little prince, you were frightened...

I'll be a lot more frightened this evening.

Once again, I was frozen by that sense of something that can't be mended. And I realized I couldn't bear the idea of never hearing his laughter again.

Tonight, it'll be one year.

My star will be right above the spot where I came down a year ago.

Little prince, isn't this just a bad dream, this story about a snake and a meeting and a star...

[c

101

That night, I didn't see him set off. He'd escaped without a sound.

When I caught up with him, he simply said to me:

Ah! You're here...

And he took me by the hand.

You shouldn't have come. It'll upset you. I'll look dead, but I won't be really.

It's too far, you see. And I can't take this body with me. It's too heavy.

But it'll be like an old skin that's been shed. It's not sad.

I'll look at the stars as well. And all the stars will be like wells with rusty pulleys.

All the stars will pour me water to drink.

102

But I didn't say anything.

And he didn't say anything either, because he was crying.

It's just there. Let me walk on my own.

And he sat down, because he was afraid.

You know ... I'm responsible for my flower. And she's so weak, and so naive. All she's got are four tiny little thorns to protect her from the world.

I sat down because I couldn't stand up any longer.

This is it now.

He hesitated a moment longer before getting up again. He took one step.

I couldn't move.

There was just a flash of yellow by his ankle.

He fell, gently as a falling tree.

He didn't even make a sound

because of the sand.

107

And now, of course, it's been six years already.

I've never told this story before. My friends were just happy to see me alive again.

I was sad, but I told them: "I'm tired, that's all."

I know the little prince made it back to his planet, because I didn't find his body at daybreak.

His muzzle!

I forgot to add the leather strap.

He'll never be able to fasten it on to his sheep.

What happened on his planet?

Perhaps the sheep really did eat the flower...

But then I think:

Surely not.

Every night, the little prince puts his flower away under her glass dome, and he watches over his sheep.

So I'm happy. And all the stars laugh softly.

Then I think: Everyone's absent-minded once in a while, and that's all it takes! One evening, he forgets the glass dome, or else the sheep escapes at night without making a noise.

And those tinkling stars change to tears.

Nothing in the universe can be the same if somewhere – nobody knows where – a sheep we've never seen may or may not have eaten a rose.

Look at the sky.

Ask yourself: Has the sheep eaten the flower, yes or no?

And you'll see

how everything changes.

And no grown-up will ever understand

how important that is.

For me, this is the most beautiful and the saddest landscape in the world.

It's the same landscape as on the page before, but I've drawn it again to show you properly. This is where the little prince appeared on the Earth, and then disappeared.

Look carefully at this landscape so you'll be able to recognize it one day if you travel to Africa, to the desert. And if you happen to pass this way, please don't be in a hurry. Wait for a while under the star!

And if a child comes to you, if he laughs, if he has golden hair, if he doesn't answer your questions, you'll be able to guess who it is.

So be kind! Don't leave me feeling sad like this.

Write quickly to let me know that he's come back...

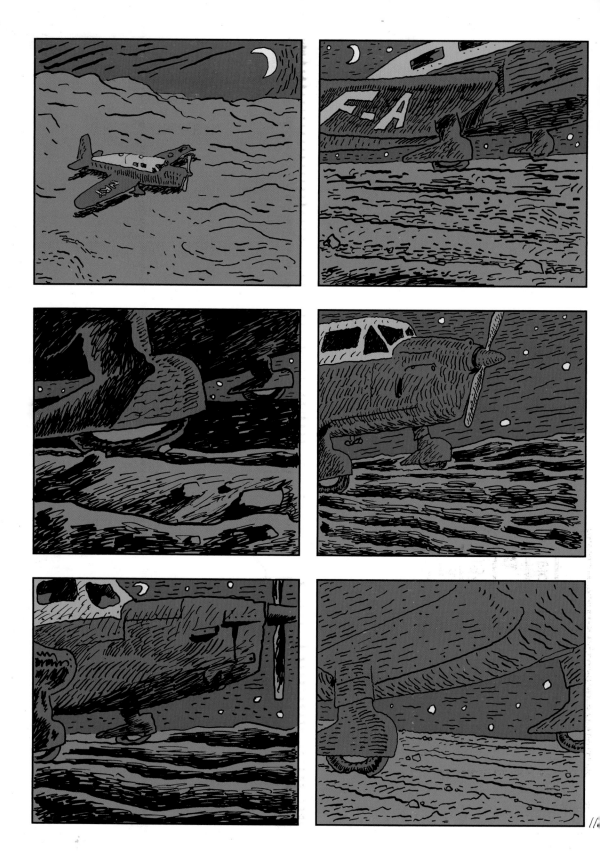